Sno
Surprise Puppy

Luke's mom shook her head. "Whoever would leave a young pup like him alone in the snow?" she said.

Luke cuddled the wriggling puppy. "Snowy's cold," he said. "And he seems really hungry. Can we take him home and give him some of Cassie's dog food?"

Luke's mom looked at Snowy, then nodded. "But we can't keep him," she warned. "We only have room for Cassie."

Snowy the
Surprise Puppy

by Jenny Dale

Illustrated by Susan Hellard

SCHOLASTIC INC.

New York   Toronto   London   Auckland   Sydney
Mexico City   New Delhi   Hong Kong   Buenos Aires

ISBN 0-439-79124-3

36 35 34 33 32 31 30 29   17 18 19 20

Printed in the U.S.A.
First printing, November 2005

Chapter One

"Wait for me!" barked the small brown puppy. His stubby legs moved quickly as he ran after the other dogs. But big Barney and Beano didn't wait.

"Smell that?" woofed Barney over his shoulder. "Fried chicken in the garbage can over there! Got to get there fast or some other dog will eat it."

The puppy sniffed the delicious smell coming from the garbage can. "Oh, save some for me!" he barked.

By the time he caught up with the two bigger dogs, they had gobbled all but one small piece.

"This is for you," woofed Beano.

"Thanks, Beano! I couldn't have reached the can on my own." The chicken was still warm and tasty. But it didn't fill the puppy's rumbling tummy.

The pup looked up at Beano and Barney. Perhaps they would look for more food. "Where now?" he barked.

"Back to the den," woofed Barney. "I smell snow on the way."

"Snow? What's snow?" asked the puppy as they made their way back to their shelter in the woods.

"It's a cold thing," woofed Beano.

"The kind of cold thing that makes me wish I still lived indoors," added Barney.

The puppy looked up at the big dog. "Have you really lived indoors, Barney?" he woofed. He'd often watched dogs out in the park, playing with their people. He wondered what it was like to have a person and live in a house.

"I used to live with a very friendly old lady," woofed Barney. "She and I lived in a warm house and she fed me and brushed me and took me for walks. She is the one who named me Barney."

"I wish I had a name," said the pup. "But why don't you live with your old lady now, Barney?"

Barney snuffled sadly. "She died. And I couldn't stay in our house on my own. So the yellow van came and took me to the animal shelter."

"I've seen that yellow van," the puppy yapped. "It sometimes drives around looking for dogs to catch, doesn't it?"

"That's right," agreed Barney.

"They take in homeless dogs and look after them."

The pup was panting now. It was hard for him to keep up with the two big dogs; his legs were so much shorter. "What's it . . . like . . . in the . . . animal shelter?" he woofed breathlessly.

Barney looked down at the pup. "It's warm and there's plenty of food and the people there like dogs," he woofed back. "But it's not the same as having your *own* home. So I escaped."

That night, it grew even colder. Under a bush in the woods, the three dogs huddled together. Beano and Barney let the pup wriggle between the two of them so that he would keep warm.

"Tell me more about living with people," the pup snuffled from his cozy place.

"Well," woofed Beano, "one of the nicest times is Christmas."

"Christmas? What's that?" The puppy yawned.

Beano put a big soft paw over the pup. "I'm not exactly sure," he woofed. "But I remember that an old man with a white beard visits. And he brings whatever you want most."

"That's right," woofed Barney. "And it's almost Christmas now. You can tell because of the pretty lights all over town."

"And the huge tree with pretty lights that grew overnight in the town square," Beano added.

The pup sighed happily, *Oh, good!* he thought. *I'm glad it's almost Christmas. I know what I want most: I want a name! And I want a person of my own . . . and a home . . . and lots to eat . . . and . . .* He yawned and closed his eyes. Then, full of hope, he fell asleep.

When the pup opened his eyes
the next morning, the world had
turned white. "What?" he barked.
"What's happened?"

Barney lifted his head to see.
Then he sighed and snuggled
back down. "Snow," he woofed.
"Stay close and we might
keep warm."

"But I want to explore!" the pup
woofed back. He scrambled away
from the others and trotted over
to the edge of the den.

He gave the white stuff a sniff.
It didn't smell like much of
anything.

He gave it a lick — and jumped
back in surprise. He'd never
tasted anything so cold!

He went back and licked the snow again. How odd! It turned to water on his tongue!

And then he was off! He jumped like a rabbit through the soft cold whiteness, his ears flapping and his tail spinning. "This is great!" he barked.

"It's not *that* exciting," complained Beano.

"Yes, it is!" the pup barked back.

"Look at that!" Behind the pup was a loopy trail of pawprints.

He ran back to the shelter and gently tugged on Barney's ear. "Come on," he yapped. "Let's play a game!"

Barney slowly stood up and shook himself. "All right," he agreed. "Just for a little while." He nudged Beano with his nose. "Come on, Beano. Shake a leg. Let's play with the little one for a while. He's never seen snow before — it's special for him."

Beano sighed. Then he, too, got up. He stretched long and hard, then bounded out into the snow.

The pup spun around, chasing his stubby tail in excitement. "I know!" he barked. "I'll run off

10

and hide. Then you follow my tracks and come and find me!"

"Oh, all right," woofed Beano.

The puppy raced off through the trees and hid behind a big holly bush.

It didn't take the big dogs long to find him.

"Happy now?" woofed Barney.

"One more turn — please!" yapped the pup. He'd never had such fun! "Just once more! I'll close my eyes and you and Beano run away this time."

The pup rolled over and over in the snow while Barney and Beano ran off into the woods. "One roll, two rolls, three rolls . . ." he snuffled.

His heart was thumping with

excitement. Where would his big friends hide? "Four rolls, five rolls, six . . ."

Suddenly, the pup heard woofing in the distance. It was Barney and Beano. And the sound came from the edge of the woods, near the road. He stopped rolling and scrambled to his feet. "Oh, Barney! Beano!" he yapped. "You've spoiled the game now!" He knew where they were hiding without even looking at their big pawprints in the snow.

As he stood there, the pup's tummy rumbled. He'd been so excited about the snow, he'd forgotten how hungry he was.

"Barney! Beano! I know where you are!" he barked. "Coming,

ready or not!" And he ran through the tracks, toward his friends.

But as the pup galloped along, the barking suddenly stopped. He heard a door banging, then an engine noise. He grew worried. What was happening?

He was almost at the edge of the woods now, where Barney and Beano's barking had come from. The dogs were no longer there. And, turning onto the big road lined with houses, was a yellow van. The animal shelter's van . . .

"Barney! Beano!" the frightened pup barked. His friends' pawprints suddenly ended. And, nearby, a person's began. It was clear. Beano and Barney had gone

to the shelter. They'd gone for food and warmth. And for the thing they called Christmas.

The pup sat down in the tire tracks and shivered. Then he howled, "If only they'd taken me!"

Chapter Two

The pup didn't want to stay in the woods on his own. He felt very cold and miserable.

He followed the tire tracks out onto the road. Perhaps he should follow them all the way to the animal shelter.

But just then, a big truck came

roaring along. Scared, the pup ran back into the edge of the woods. And when he came out again, the tracks were gone — squashed by the huge wheels of the truck.

He sat down in the snow again and whimpered, "*What* will I do *now*?"

An excited shout came from one of the houses nearby. A boy came running out into the snow. An elderly golden retriever trotted slowly behind him. "Come on, Cassie," the boy shouted. "Come and play!"

The pup thought the boy looked like lots of fun. He watched as the boy scooped up a handful of snow, made it into a ball, then threw it.

Ears pricked and alert, the pup stood up again. He wanted to play, too! He wanted to run and catch the snowball. But he knew that it was meant for the big golden dog called Cassie. So he stayed where he was and just yapped, "Go on! Catch it, Cassie!"

But Cassie didn't run. She stood and watched the snowball drop to the ground.

What a waste! the pup thought.

The boy's mother came out. She patted Cassie on the head and told the boy, "Don't make Cassie play if she doesn't want to, Luke. She's missing Grandpa too much to feel like playing."

Luke looked disappointed, but he nodded, then took something out of his pocket. He held it out. "Here, Cassie!" he called.

But it wasn't Cassie that came. It was a ball of brown fur covered with snowflakes that shot toward Luke.

"Is that food you've got in your hand?" the pup barked. He leaped up, yapping and panting.

"Hey!" laughed Luke. He was so surprised that he lost his

balance and fell over into the snow. He dropped the dog biscuit he'd held out for Cassie, and the pup quickly grabbed it.

Luke watched the puppy crunch on the biscuit. "I wonder who he belongs to," he said to his mom.

The pup ran over to Luke and

licked his face, wagging his tail hard. "I don't belong to anyone!" he yapped. "I could be yours — and we could play together forever, if you want!"

Luke was laughing too much to move, but at last he pushed the wriggling, snow-covered puppy aside and stood up. "Hey, Snowy, I like you," he said.

"I like you, too!" yapped the puppy. "And I like the name you've given me — Snowy! If you've given me a name, then that must mean I belong to you now. Great!"

Luke's mom shook her head. "Whoever would leave a young pup like him alone in the snow?" she said.

Luke cuddled the wriggling puppy. "Snowy's cold," he said. "And he seems really hungry. Can we take him home and give him some of Cassie's dog food?"

Luke's mom looked at Snowy, then nodded. "But we can't keep him," she warned. "We only have room for Cassie."

Snowy's heart sank. He gave Luke's cheek a sorrowful lick.

"After we've fed him, he'll have to go to the animal shelter," Luke's mom added.

Snowy's ears pricked up a little. He looked at Luke. "I'd rather stay with you," he yapped. "But at least my friends Barney and Beano are at the shelter." He gave his tail a little wag.

Chapter Three

As Luke's mom opened the door of their home, warm air wrapped around Snowy like a blanket, snug and welcoming.

He followed Luke and Cassie into a room full of delicious food smells. His mouth began to water as Luke emptied food from a can into a bowl.

"Dad!" Luke shouted. "Come and see what we've found!" He put the bowl on the floor.

Snowy ran straight to the bowl and gobbled the food as fast as he could. He'd learned from Beano and Barney that you must eat anything you find as fast as you can. Otherwise, some other dog might push you out of the way and eat it for you!

He looked up at Cassie. She was much bigger than he was. Perhaps she would push him out of the way to gobble the food herself.

To his surprise, Snowy saw that the big old dog was watching

him eat. But her eyes were gentle.
She didn't seem interested in
having any of the food herself. "Is
all this for me?" Snowy yapped.

"It is," Cassie woofed kindly.

Soon, all the food was inside
Snowy. Tummy full, Snowy
yawned a happy yawn that
turned into a burp!

A man's voice laughed. "Well,
he's made himself at home — and

wherever he's come from, they've forgotten to teach him any manners!"

Snowy looked up and saw a tall man smiling down at him.

"Oh, Dad! He's only a little puppy." Luke squatted down to stroke Snowy's brown head.

Snowy wagged his tail and licked Luke's hand. Then he jumped up and licked Luke's chin.

"Isn't he great?" Luke laughed. "Couldn't we keep him, Dad?"

Luke's dad shook his head. "Not while we've got Cassie, son," he said. "Come and give me a hand to finish the decorations. Then we'll take that little fellow to the shelter, okay?"

"I suppose so," said Luke. But

he sounded disappointed. And so was Snowy.

Luke's house wasn't quite how Snowy had expected a house to be. There was a tree growing inside one of the rooms! So the inside world wasn't so very different from the woods, after all. "It's a little like my old den," he yapped. "But I haven't seen leaves like those before." There were bright, shiny shapes on some of the branches.

"Do you like the decorations?" Luke asked Snowy.

Snowy was nosing around in a box full of bright colors and strange objects.

"Hey, get that puppy out of there!" said Luke's dad.

Snowy watched Luke put the box of decorations up high on a table. Still, there were chains of colored paper to chase and pounce on. Snowy skidded across the wooden floor and landed in a tangle of paper chain. It hung like a garland around his neck.

Luke laughed and picked up an end of the chain.

"Hurrah!" barked Snowy. "I've seen one of these before — it's a leash. And Luke's on the other end of it, so that must mean he's my person after all!"

But Snowy was wrong.

"Sorry, Snowy," Luke told him. "Time to go to the shelter." Luke picked the puppy up and carried him out of the cozy house.

Cassie's gentle eyes watched from the doorway, and Luke's mom gave Snowy a fond pat as he left with Luke and his dad.

Oh, well, thought Snowy. He felt sad, but at least he'd be back with Barney and Beano. And besides, he had an idea. He wriggled in Luke's arms and turned to look at him. "It will be

Christmas in the shelter, won't
it?" he yapped. "And I'll still get
what I want most in the world,
won't I?"

Luke didn't answer. He just held
Snowy to his cheek and whispered,
"I'll really miss you, Snowy."

"It's all right," Snowy snuffled
in Luke's ear. "Barney told me
that at Christmas you get
whatever you want most. I want
you most! So we'll be back
together again soon!"

But Luke didn't seem to
understand. He still looked sad
as they arrived at the animal
shelter and rang the bell.

"We've brought a puppy we
found in the snow," Luke's
dad said.

But the man at the door shook his head. "Two strays from the woods have been brought in today," he explained.

"Yes, that's Barney and Beano!" Snowy woofed in agreement.

"And they took the last two places," the man went on. "We're all full up now. So you can't leave that pup here, I'm afraid."

"What?" yapped Snowy, feeling frightened again. Not stay with Luke *or* Barney and Beano? "I don't want to be on my own!" he whimpered.

Snowy looked at Luke. "You've got to do something, Luke," he cried. "You're my person now. It's your job to save me!"

Chapter Four

Luke looked at the frightened
puppy in his arms. He turned to
his father. "We'll just have to take
him home again, Dad."

Luke's dad frowned. "But,
Luke, we've already got Cassie."

"Dad, pleeeease!" Luke
pleaded.

Luke's dad reached out and gave Snowy a stroke. The puppy licked his hand. Luke's dad smiled. "Okay. I can see we'll have a miserable Christmas if we don't take him home with us."

"So we can keep him?" Luke's face beamed happiness.

"For Christmas, yes," said his dad. "But once there's room in the shelter, that's where he must go."

"At least we'll have Christmas together! Awesome!" Luke yelled. He hugged Snowy, who yapped his delight, too.

Luke's dad covered his ears and laughed. "This could be an interesting Christmas," he said.

*   *   *

Back home, Luke made a bed for
Snowy out of the empty
Christmas-decorations box and
an old blanket. Then he put the
box next to Cassie's big basket on
the kitchen floor.

"Come on, Snowy!" he called.
"Try out your new bed."

But Snowy was far too excited
to think about sleep. There were

so many places and things to explore in his new indoor world.

"What's that puppy up to now?" asked Luke's mom.

Luke quickly took the glove that Snowy was tasting and put it out of the pup's reach.

"I was enjoying that!" Snowy whined.

"Lucky for you, Mom's getting new gloves for Christmas!" Luke told Snowy. He pointed to one of the gift boxes under the tree in the living room. "You must behave yourself, Snowy, or Mom and Dad won't want you around!"

Snowy did try to behave. It wasn't really his fault that he got in Luke's dad's way as he carried in logs for the fire. The house was so crowded.

"How is it that Cassie is ten times Snowy's size, and yet Cassie manages to keep out of the way?" Luke's dad asked, shaking his head.

And when the strange leaves on the indoor tree suddenly became bright lights, Snowy was so excited that, somehow, he pulled the whole tree over!

"Snowy!" Luke ran to put the tree upright again.

Luke's dad heard the clatter and came into the room. "What's that pup been up to now?" he asked.

"He was just admiring the tree lights," said Luke, brushing pine needles off his pants.

"I see," said his dad, smiling. "Maybe a run in the yard would do both of you good before dinner."

Luke and Snowy ran outside together, shouting and barking and chasing each other over the snow. Cassie followed them to the doorway and sat watching, her tail swishing softly.

When they all went inside again, there was a new brightly wrapped box under the tree, and it had Luke's name on it.

"Look at this, Snowy. It's a present for me!" Luke said.

"I wonder what it is," snuffled Snowy, sniffing at the box. "I'm afraid it doesn't smell very interesting."

Luke sat on the floor and pulled the puppy onto his lap. "I think it's a game," he said.

"And is that what you want most in the world?" Snowy woofed. He licked Luke's ear. "Barney told me that you get what you want most in the world at Christmas."

But Luke didn't answer.

Snowy didn't want to sleep that night. Perhaps if he closed his eyes, his new indoor world would disappear.

Cassie nudged the puppy with her big nose. "Go to sleep, little one," she woofed softly. "Luke will still be here in the morning."

Snowy yawned, "Okay." Then

he looked up at the old dog. She seemed so sad. "Why are you so unhappy, Cassie?" he asked.

"Oh, there's someone I'm missing," Cassie woofed back. "Nothing for you to worry about." Then she curled around and around in her bed and settled down for sleep.

"Cassie," Snowy went on, "my friends told me that an old man with a white beard brings you whatever you want on Christmas Day. And that's tomorrow, isn't it?"

But there was no answer. Cassie began to snore softly.

Snowy sighed and settled down, too. Perhaps he could ask the old man if he could help Cassie as well.

Chapter Five

"Merry Christmas!" Luke came into the kitchen, still dressed in his pajamas.

"Christmas? Is this Christmas?" Snowy barked. He jumped up at Luke and licked his hand. "Hooray! The man who makes wishes come true is coming today!"

Luke's dad came in. "Merry Christmas!" he called. "So, I wonder what Santa Claus has brought you, Luke?"

"Lots!" said Luke, smiling happily. "There are loads more gifts under the tree than there were when I went to bed last night!"

Snowy stopped jumping around. He looked up at Luke in dismay. "Santa Claus? You mean the man who makes wishes come true? He's already been here? And I've missed him? Oh, no!" he whimpered.

Luke turned to look at the pup. "What's the matter, boy?" he said. He bent down and picked Snowy up to give him a cuddle.

"Luke, why don't you go and get dressed, while I feed the dogs?" his dad said. "Then you can take them out into the yard while I make breakfast."

Luke nodded. "Yes," he said. "Snowy and I have to make the most of the time we've got together."

Snowy managed to forget his disappointment at missing Santa Claus when the presents were opened. He was an expert at getting inside wrappers and boxes. Beano and Barney had shown him how you could find food inside some of them. And he'd found all sorts of delicious-smelling things for Luke in his packages.

Snowy and Cassie even had their own gifts. A whole bag of dog biscuits for each of them!

"Help me with this one, Snowy," said Luke as he tore paper off a big box. It was a baseball and a baseball jersey.

"You have the clothes and I'll have the ball," yapped Snowy. He nosed the ball under a chair. But

then he couldn't get it out. Luke laughed.

Snowy raced over to help Luke's mom open one of her boxes. He dragged out a new pink slipper for her. "This looks very chewy!" he yapped.

"Not for you!" laughed Luke's mother as she took it from him.

When all the presents were unwrapped, there was a huge pile of bright crumpled paper in the middle of the floor. Snowy pushed his nose into the paper, then rolled around, having a great time.

"He's trying to wrap himself up!" laughed Luke's mom. She opened Snowy's bag of dog biscuits and gave him one.

"Thanks!" Snowy snuffled through a mouthful of biscuit. He wasn't really hungry. He and Cassie had each been given a big bowl of meat and crunchy little biscuits for breakfast. But he made an effort and finished the biscuit to be polite.

"Leave some room for Christmas dinner, boy!" Luke laughed.

Snowy wagged his tail again. He'd hardly stopped wagging it all morning. *I like Christmas,* he thought. *And I love living here with Luke!*

Then his tail drooped as he remembered. *If only I'd stayed awake to meet Santa Claus,* he thought. *Then I could have asked*

him to make it all right for me to stay
with Luke forever.

Luke's mom was busy in the
kitchen. Snowy watched her
chopping and stirring things that
smelled wonderful. He'd
changed his mind about not
being hungry!
   "Where's Dad gone?"
asked Luke.
   "Oh, just to collect something
for dinner," his mom said
quickly. "Could you set the
table, please, Luke?"
   Snowy kept close to Luke's
ankles as he went back and forth
between the cupboard and the
table.

"Careful, boy, you'll trip me up!" Luke said.

But Snowy wasn't going to let Luke disappear while he wasn't looking. He'd lost Barney and Beano — and he'd missed Santa Claus. He was going to keep a much closer eye on Luke.

"Here, Cassie, there's a good old girl. Here, Snowy! Come on, boy!" called Luke's mom a while later.

Cassie ambled out into the kitchen.

"Go on, Snowy — go and have your Christmas dinner!" said Luke. "I'll still be here when you've finished!"

Snowy got a sudden sniff of sausage from the kitchen, and his mouth began to water. "Well, if you're sure . . ." he woofed. Then he went running after Cassie, his little paws skidding across the shiny kitchen floor.

Luke's mom had put chopped-up sausage and turkey with gravy into the dog bowls.

Even Cassie seemed to forget her sadness as she ate the

delicious treat. Her tail wagged a little.

Then a sudden sound outside made Cassie stop licking her bowl. She ran out of the kitchen and down the hallway to the front door.

"What is it?" Snowy yapped. He gave his bowl a last lick, then followed Cassie.

"It must be Dad coming home," said Luke. He opened the front door, and Snowy looked out. He sat down in surprise. Luke's dad was helping someone get out of the car. It was an old man with a white beard. Could it be Santa Claus?

Chapter Six

Maybe Snowy hadn't missed
Santa Claus after all! Even Cassie
was excited. She bounded out
through the front door and up to
the old man. Snowy hadn't seen
her move so quickly before.

Snowy followed. "Hello, Santa
Claus!" he barked. "I'm so glad

you've come back!" He ran up and tugged at the old man's long coat to get his attention. "I've got to tell you what I want more than anything in the world so you can make it come true!"

The old man bent a little stiffly and smiled at Snowy. "And who are you?" he asked. Then he laughed as, with hugs and smiles, everyone tried to tell him at once who Snowy was.

"I think you'd better come into the warmth," said Luke's mom. "We'll tell you all about Snowy over dinner."

Luke and his mom and dad and Santa Claus sat at the table. They pulled noisemakers that made

Snowy jump and bark in surprise.

They ate big platefuls of wonderful-smelling food. Santa Claus reached secretly under the table to give Cassie and Snowy a few treats from his plate.

That proves who he is! thought Snowy. He licked his lips after

swallowing some tasty roasted potato.

Luke told the old man how he and Cassie had found the pup in the snow and given him his name. Then he explained how there was no room for Snowy at the animal shelter.

"And I just wish I could keep him forever," said Luke quietly.

Santa Claus looked down at Cassie. "There's no better friend than a good dog," he said. And Snowy almost burst with yaps when he heard that. Santa Claus understood!

"I know, Grandpa," Luke said.

Grandpa? Snowy looked at Cassie, puzzled. "Luke's grandpa is Santa Claus?" he yapped.

Cassie flopped down and put her front paws over her eyes. "No, silly!" she sighed. "He's not Santa Claus. I would have told you, but you were too excited to listen!"

Snowy's tail drooped. Not Santa Claus!

"He's Luke's grandpa — and *my* person," Cassie woofed, her tail wagging happily. "He's been very sick, in the hospital. And no one knew if he'd be well enough to come home for Christmas — until today!"

She got up and gave her owner's hand a lick, then settled back down again. "I'm so glad he's better. I've been miserable without him. Luke and his mom and dad are very nice — but I love Grandpa best. I can't wait to go back home with him!"

Snowy's tail rose a little. "Do you mean this isn't your home?" he yapped.

"Oh, no!" Cassie woofed back. "My home is down the road, in Grandpa's house. We're going back there tonight."

"But if you're not going to be here anymore . . ." Snowy was so excited, his yap came out as a squeak! "Then there would be room here for me!"

Just then, Luke shouted out a very loud HURRAH!

Snowy leaped out from under the table to see why.

"Snowy! Mom and Dad say

there's room for you, now that
Cassie can go home with
Grandpa!" Luke yelled.

"That's just what Cassie and I
have been talking about!" Snowy
barked back. "Hurrah! Hurrah!
Hurrah!" He spun around and
around. He was so happy, he
didn't know what else to do!

Luke got up from the table and
rushed over to Snowy and
scooped him up for a hug.

Snowy yelped with joy and
licked Luke as hard as he could.

"You'd better take Snowy and
Cassie out into the yard, Luke,"
his grandpa laughed. "They'll
need to run off some of that huge
dinner."

Cassie followed Luke and Snowy out. This time, she chased and jumped for Luke's snowballs, just like Snowy.

At first they didn't notice the grown-ups coming out in their coats.

"We're all going to walk home with Grandpa now, Luke," his mom called.

Luke stopped making snowballs and ran over to give his grandpa a hug.

The old man smiled, then gave Luke a small package.

Luke looked surprised. "What's this, Grandpa?" he asked.

"Well, it was my present for Cassie," he said. "Your mom

bought it for me while I was sick. But there's someone here who needs it more. Cassie won't mind."

Luke opened the package — and took out a beautiful yellow collar and leash. "Oh, Grandpa . . ." he said. "For Snowy . . . thank you!" And he hugged his grandpa again, hard. "It's a little big, but Snowy will grow into it."

Snowy went shyly up to Grandpa, his tail wagging softly. His own collar and leash! "I knew it — you really *are* Santa Claus," he woofed. He reached up and licked the old man's hand. Snowy knew now why Cassie loved her owner so much.

Then the old man bent down

stiffly toward Cassie and clipped on her leash. "You'll have to go slow for a bit, old girl," he said, smiling. "Until I get my strength back."

Cassie understood and walked down the path at the same gentle pace as her owner.

Luke quickly bent down and, with his dad's help, put on Snowy's new collar and leash. "You're really mine now, Snowy," he said.

"And you're mine!" Snowy yapped back.

Then they ran to catch up with Grandpa and Cassie.